Baa
for
Beginners

Near

Far

Thin

Fat

Wobbly

Calm

Shivery

Breezy

Bubbly

Ghostly

Breathless

Thanks for helping the Baa'd
Petra, Lina and Joe, Rachel and Mercedes

BAA FOR BEGINNERS

First edition for the United States and Canada published in 2005 by Barron's
Educational Series, Inc.

First published in the United Kingdom in 2005 by Hutchinson,
an imprint of Random House Children's Books
RANDOM HOUSE CHILDREN'S BOOKS
61–63 Uxbridge Road, London W5 5SA
A division of The Random House Group Ltd

All inquiries should be addressed to:
Barron's Educational Series, Inc.
250 Wireless Boulevard
Hauppauge, New York 11788
www.barronseduc.com

Library of Congress Catalog Card No. 2004108625

International Standard Book No. 0-7641-3095-1

Printed in Singapore
9 8 7 6 5 4 3 2 1

Baa
for
Beginners

Deborah Fajerman

The language of sheep is called Baa
and every single word is baa.

There are many different ways to speak Baa.

But when sheep are lambs
they only know one kind.

So their teacher Mrs. Ramsbottom
takes them on a field trip.

When Baa is near
it's loud and clear.

When Baa is far
it's hard to hear.

When a lamb is all alone,
its baa sounds small and thin . . .

But Baa sounds big
and fat when all the
lambs join in!

Baa is shivery
when it snows . . .

and is whisked right away when the wind blows.

When sheep are climbing
they don't have enough
breath to baaaa . . .

they just huff and puff and
puff and huff.

Baa sounds rather wobbly when it's dark as night.

But Baa is calm and flat
when the sun is bright.

When sheep sit on the grass
their bottoms turn bright green.

A bubble bath with bubbly baas
makes their bottoms clean.

Mrs. Ramsbottom has
finished the field trip.
It is time for the lambs
to take their Baa exam.

They all get a gold star.
And now it's time for their very best baas . . .

The ones they say to their ma's and pa's!

Near

Far

Thin

Fat

Wobbly

Calm

Shivery

Breezy

Bubbly

Ghostly

Breathless

spill damage
1/18/06 EW